THE TALE OF
MR. JEREMY FISHER

BY BEATRIX POTTER

FREDERICK WARNE

ONCE upon a time there was a frog called
Mr. Jeremy Fisher; he lived in a little damp
house amongst the buttercups at the edge
of a pond.

THE water was all slippy-sloppy in the larder and in the back passage.

But Mr. Jeremy liked getting his feet wet; nobody ever scolded him, and he never caught a cold!

8

FREDERICK WARNE

Published by the Penguin Group
Registered office: 80 Strand, London, WC2R 0RL
Penguin Young Readers Group, 345 Hudson Street, New York, N.Y. 10014, USA

First published 1906 by Frederick Warne
This edition with new reproductions of Beatrix Potter's book illustrations first published 2006
This edition copyright © Frederick Warne & Co. 2006
Reissued 2016
New reproductions of Beatrix Potter's book illustrations copyright © Frederick Warne & Co. 2002
Original copyright in text and illustrations © Frederick Warne & Co., 1906

Frederick Warne & Co. is the owner of all rights, copyrights and trademarks in the
Beatrix Potter character names and illustrations.

Manufactured in China

Special Markets ISBN 978-0-723-26002-8

HE was quite pleased when he looked out and saw large drops of rain, splashing in the pond— "I will get some worms and go fishing and catch a dish of minnows for my dinner," said Mr. Jeremy Fisher. "If I catch more than five fish, I will invite my friends Mr. Alderman Ptolemy Tortoise and Sir Isaac Newton. The Alderman, however, eats salad."

MR. JEREMY put on a macintosh, and a
pair of shiny goloshes; he took his rod and
basket, and set off with enormous hops to
the place where he kept his boat.

THE boat was round and green, and very
like the other lily-leaves. It was tied to a
water-plant in the middle of the pond.

MR. JEREMY took a reed pole, and pushed the boat out into open water. "I know a good place for minnows," said Mr. Jeremy Fisher.

Mr. Jeremy stuck his pole into the mud and fastened his boat to it.

THEN he settled himself cross-legged
and arranged his fishing tackle. He had the
dearest little red float. His rod was a tough
stalk of grass, his line was a fine long white
horse-hair, and he tied a little wriggling
worm at the end.

THE rain trickled down his back, and for nearly an hour he stared at the float.

"This is getting tiresome, I think I should like some lunch," said Mr. Jeremy Fisher.

He punted back again amongst the water-plants, and took some lunch out of his basket.

"I will eat a butterfly sandwich, and wait till the shower is over," said Mr. Jeremy Fisher.

A GREAT big water-beetle
came up underneath the lily
leaf and tweaked the toe of one
of his goloshes.

Mr. Jeremy crossed his legs up shorter, out of
reach, and went on eating his sandwich.

Once or twice something moved about
with a rustle and a splash
amongst the rushes
at the side of the
pond.

"I trust that is
not a rat," said
Mr. Jeremy
Fisher; "I think
I had better get
away from here."

MR. JEREMY shoved the boat out again a
little way, and dropped in the bait. There was
a bite almost directly; the float gave a
tremendous bobbit!

"A minnow! a minnow! I have him by the
nose!" cried Mr. Jeremy Fisher, jerking up
his rod.

BUT what a horrible surprise! Instead of a smooth fat minnow, Mr. Jeremy landed little Jack Sharp the stickleback, covered with spines!
  The stickleback floundered about the boat, pricking and snapping until he was quite out of breath. Then he jumped back into the water.

AND a shoal of other little fishes put their heads out, and laughed at Mr. Jeremy Fisher.

AND while Mr. Jeremy sat disconsolately on the edge of his boat—sucking his sore fingers and peering down into the water—a *much* worse thing happened; a really *frightful* thing it would have been, if Mr. Jeremy had not been wearing a macintosh!

A GREAT big enormous trout came up—
ker-pflop-p-p-p! with a splash—and it seized
Mr. Jeremy with a snap, "Ow! Ow! Ow!"— and
then it turned and dived down to the bottom of
the pond!

But the trout was so displeased with the taste
of the macintosh, that in less
than half a minute it
spat him out again;
and the only thing
it swallowed was
Mr. Jeremy's
goloshes.

MR. JEREMY bounced
up to the surface of the
water, like a cork and
the bubbles out of
a soda water bottle;
and he swam with all
his might to the edge
of the pond.

He scrambled out on the
first bank he came to,
and he hopped home
across the meadow
with his macintosh
all in tatters.

"WHAT a mercy that was not a pike!" said
Mr. Jeremy Fisher. "I have lost my rod and
basket; but it does not much matter, for I am
sure I should never have dared to go fishing
again!"

HE put some sticking plaster on his fingers, and his friends both came to dinner. He could not offer them fish, but he had something else in his larder.

SIR ISAAC NEWTON wore his black and
gold waistcoat,

AND Mr. Alderman Ptolemy Tortoise
brought a salad with him in a string bag.

AND instead of a nice dish of minnows—they had a roasted grasshopper with ladybird sauce; which frogs consider a beautiful treat; but *I* think it must have been nasty.